To Katie, Ben & George
—D.L.

The illustrations in this book were created with pen, pencil crayons, watercolor paints, and Photoshop.

Cataloging-in-Publication Data has been applied for and may be obtained from the Library of Congress.

ISBN 978-1-4197-3318-5

First published by Frances Lincoln Children's Books, an imprint of the Quarto Group, in September 2017

Printed and bound in China
10 9 8 7 6 5 4 3 2 1

Abrams Books for Young Readers are available at special discounts when purchased in quantity for premiums and promotions as well as fundraising or educational use. Special editions can also be created to specification. For details, contact specialsales@abramsbooks.com or the address below.

ABRAMS The Art of Books
195 Broadway, New York, NY 10007
abramsbooks.com

THE BOY
AND THE
GIANT

David Litchfield

Abrams Books for Young Readers
New York

The townspeople of faraway Gableview were friendly and bright. They painted the wall surrounding their town with a mural, welcoming visitors from near and far.

But Little Billy was in a pickle.

"Grandad," he said. "How will we finish the mural?
No one can reach the top of the wall."

"Don't worry!" said Grandad.

"I know just the fellow who can help . . ."

"He has legs as long as drainpipes," Grandad
continued, "hands the size of tabletops, and feet as
big as rowboats . . ."

"The Secret Giant," Billy sighed. "I've heard a thousand stories
about him, Grandad, from you and everyone else in Gableview.
But those aren't real—they're just legends!"

"How can you forget all the times the Giant helped us out?"
Grandad asked.

"When we went camping last summer, it was the Giant who kept the bears away."

"And when the town clock stopped chiming,
it was the Giant who fixed it."

"And when our fishing boat got caught in the storm, it was the Giant who pulled us safely to shore."

stopped the big oak from falling in the wind,

helped cars cross the bridge when part of it fell down,

caught your favorite kite before it blew away,

and rescued Murphy when he got stuck on the roof.

The Giant did all these things for the people of
Gableview, quietly and without making a fuss."

"But that's *impossible*, Grandad," Billy said. "I didn't see a giant *any* of those times! I didn't see any legs as long as drainpipes or hands the size of tabletops or feet as big as rowboats!"

"Maybe you weren't looking hard enough," Grandad replied. "Or maybe the Giant didn't want you to see him."

"But that's silly, Grandad!" Billy argued. "If this Giant is so great, why would he hide?"

"Because people are scared of things that are different. And sometimes, they're not so nice. Try getting up and going to the mural tomorrow at dawn," Grandad suggested. "If you keep an open mind, I think you'll be surprised by what you find."

Billy went to sleep, forgetting all about Grandad's silly stories. He dreamed of fishing and camping and flying kites—but no Giant!

Billy woke up at dawn to the sound of Murphy's barking. When Billy took him out for a walk, Murphy led them down the main road to the town mural.

"Don't be silly, boy," said Billy as they
turned the corner.
"There's no such thing as a . . ."

"G—G—GIANT!"

He WAS real! With legs as long as drainpipes and hands the size of tabletops and feet as big as rowboats…

…and he was

TERRIFYING!

Billy ran away.

As fast as he could.

But then he remembered
what Grandad had said
about people being
scared of things that are
different.

Billy turned back . . .

But the Giant had gone.

Billy went home and told Grandad what had happened.
"I shouldn't have run away," Billy said sadly.

"You were right, Grandad! The Giant stays hidden away because people are afraid of him. He doesn't feel welcome in Gableview. And now I've just made it worse."

"Well, I'm sure you can think of a way to make the Giant feel better," said Grandad. "What makes you feel better when you're upset?"

Billy had a great idea.

They got to work.

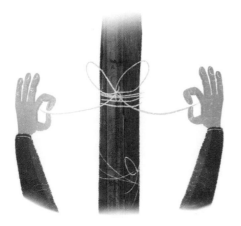

They climbed up high on the scaffold and worked hard all day to make the Giant a present he would never forget.

Then there was nothing
to do but wait . . .

and wait some more.

They waited all afternoon,
until the sun began to set.

"What if the Giant doesn't come back?" Billy said. "Maybe I've hurt his feelings so badly that he doesn't want to live in Gableview at all anymore!"

But then . . .

They saw legs as long as drainpipes, hands the size of tabletops, and feet as large as rowboats.

IT WAS THE GIANT!

The Giant saw his present.
For the first time since comings to Gableview,
the Giant smiled.

What Billy realized is that the Giant wasn't just a giant. He was also a person. A person to be welcomed, just like the other visitors to Gableview from near and far.

WELCOME TO GABLEVIEW

And he wanted what everyone
wanted when they were upset.

A friend.